Tragic:

Tomorrow is Never Promised

ISBN: 979-8323931316
ISBN-13: 979-8323931316

Library of Congress Cataloging-in-Publication Data

Karter, Darrow
T.R.A.G.I.C.: Tomorrow is Never Promised.
TXu002414192 / 2024-02-05

Published by Dey'Vonna Publishing, Dallas, TX

Manufactured in the United States of America

Acknowledgment

I want to acknowledge the love of my life for always pushing me to do better. I also want to acknowledge my close friend/sister Jay for believing in me even when I didn't believe in myself.

I want to acknowledge my grandma for instilling in me ever since I was a child that no MATTER WHAT YOU are GOING THROUGH, NEVER LET THEM SEE YOU SWEAT.

I also would like to acknowledge my big bro for making me understand every second is counted AS LONG AS YOU GOT BREATH IN YOUR BODY. THERE'S TIME TO MAKE ANOTHER DOLLAR TO PROVIDE FOR YOUR FAMILY.

And lastly, Y'all know I can't forget my strength. Everything I do is for my daughter....I love y'all.

At a red light, I was in traffic sitting in the turning lane; the arrow appeared green, giving me the right of way. As I made a left, I eased on the gas pedal; the sun was out, and people were out.

"*You should have made a right,*" a voice came from the back seat. I looked into the rear-view mirror and noticed the sun was no longer beaming. It was gone, and the moon was out; the light blue skies suddenly darkened into midnight blue skies, the half-moon began to turn into a full moon, and the voice from the backseat became a reflection of me staring right into my own eyes. I wasn't scared, but I did lose focus on where I was headed. *"Can I ask you a question?"* My reflection asked myself; "of course," I answered. *"Would you have cried today if you were to die tomorrow?"* **BOOM, BOOM, Boom,** three gunshots sound off before I can answer the question.

As I entered the gas station, I heard sirens and saw blue and red lights. A squad car, then another squad car, began to fly by the gas station at a high rate of speed. I walked back to my car and headed towards the commotion. As I wandered down this familiar block, I passed by people standing around, some crying, some screaming, some angry, while others stood in disbelief from all the drama. I looked up towards the skies and stared into the full moon; I proceeded towards the body on the ground, praying it was no one I knew. I looked down and saw myself on the ground, shot. I stared at my dead body; it was like an out-of-body body experience.

The eyes of my lifeless body began to open, and I started soul-gazing within myself. My mouth began to open, and as my lips moved, my body said, "Better yet, if you knew you were going to die today, would you have cried yesterday?" I then awake.

7:37 A.M.

I awoke to my phone going off; I opened my eyes to sunlight beaming through my bedroom window. I reached over to grab my phone beside my bed on my nightstand, and "7 Driver Larry" flashed across the screen. This was my 4th year running my own moving truck company, and Larry is one of my drivers. "Hello," I said. "How are you doing this morning, Larry," I asked. "I'm great, how about you," I asked. "I'm great; I'm just calling to report that when I stepped out of the house this morning, one of the tires was flat on the truck. I already called AAA, and they are on their way now. I just wanted to let you know that I'm going to be a little behind on the pick-up and drop-off this morning," he said. "OK, I appreciate you updating me; it seems you have everything under control. Call the customer and tell them you are running late," I instructed him. He responded, "OK, will do." I hung up and headed towards the washroom to take care of my early morning doings.

I smelled breakfast directions in the air; I changed directions and headed toward the kitchen. As I walked inside, I saw my wife standing at the hot stove, "hey babe, good morning," I said. "Where is Gabby," I asked. My wife, Tonya, and I have been married for five years, and we have one child named Gabby; she is 17 years old and in her senior year of high school. "Good morning honey, Gabby should be almost dressed for school. I saw her come out of the bathroom too long ago."

"Well, I know you are happy. Today is your fifth day and Friday. I got something planned for us this weekend, but first thing in the morning, I'm taking Mamma and Gabby out to breakfast so you can rest until you feel like getting up," I said as I kissed her on her mouth. "Boy, your breath smells like shake that ass in overdrive and overtime," Tonya said, laughing. I couldn't do anything but laugh and smile as I walked out of the kitchen and into the bathroom.

8:52 A.M.

In front of Gabby's high school, I pulled up to the light at 79th and Pulaski. "Do you want me to pick you up after school, or do you have other plans?" "No, I don't have other plans; you could pick me up? But if things change, I will call you and let you know", she responded as she scanned through her phone. "Well, have a great day and learn something," I said as I pulled out $40 and handed it to her as she exited the car. I waited until she entered the school before I pulled off.

I had not even made it past Daley College before my phone began vibrating; I noticed it was one of my childhood friends, Shardo, who was also a customer of mine. Even though I have been legit for a few years, I still had one foot in the streets. "Yooo, what's good my nigga? You in traffic," he asked. I responded to him, "You know I had to drop Gabby off at school; what are you trying to get into?" He replied, "You know if I'm jumping through this early, I'm worm searching, same thing as last time. Do you want me to pull up to your crib?" I responded to him, "Yeah, bro, OK, give me twenty minutes." The call ended.

9:15 A. M.

I finally pulled up to Shardo's crib; as I parked my car, I texted him, *"I'm out here, come out."* He replied, *"The door is unlocked; just come in."* Once inside, I sat 504g on the kitchen table. I noticed he already had everything ready to cook up. He poured the raw coke into the glass pot and asked, "When did you last talk to Keazy?"

Keazy is also one of our close childhood friends incarcerated at Cook County Correctional Facility, fighting a first-degree murder charge. He has been there going on for four years now. "Bro usually calls me every couple of days, but it's been four days now; why you ask that?" "I haven't talked to bro in a while; I think his bitch ass mad at me, he continued. "What makes you think that?" I said as I stared him into his eyes. "He called me and asked me for some bread; I told him I got him but never got around to it. Days after that, he called back, but I was in the middle of some shit, so I couldn't answer.

No lie that rubbed me the wrong way." I wanted to say all types of shit, but this is what came out, "Man, you wild as hell! Keazy in the middle of some shit. Bro going through it in that bitch, you can't answer the phone for a nigga. You claim you got love for Bro; I got all types of shit going on, and I never miss Bro's call. So don't give me that shit; that's fucked up; yo ass makes money all day, every day, so what you can give me is a couple of dollars for

Bro right now. I'm going to match it and make sure he gets it today." Shardo went into his pockets and handed me $200.00. I responded to him, "What the fuck is this Bro? Kick that shit out, Bro needs at least a nickel from you. We have to send Bro a G." Shardo laughed as he dug back into his pockets and handed me $300.00 more dollars and said, "Bro bitch ass lucky I love him; I'm gon tell Bro to hit yo line once he jumps through my shit, I have to get up out of here. I have some shit to take care of; get up with me," I said as I shook his hand before leaving.

11:40 A.M.

Hours later, I find myself doing paperwork at my place of business; I get a text on my phone from my mans Corey, "Tryna to get up with you, wya?" I texted back, "At work, give me an hour." He replied, "That's cool, just let me know." Not even an hour later, I walked out the door and called Corey. "How you coming," I asked. "I'm trying to get in tune with a freshman," he responded. "OK, give me fifteen minutes to get it together; where do you want to meet," I answered. He replied, "Just pull up on my block; I'm standing in front of my crib."

12:24 P.M.

As I made a right up 69th and Maplewood, the first thing that hit my nose was BBQ, then weed, music blasting, people laughing, playing, eating, and having a good time. Once I parked my car, Corey walked up and jumped in; I passed him 252g of cooked crack as he handed me my money. As I counted through the money I was just handed, I noticed all was not there, "where's my $500 you owe me, bro, off that last move?" "Damn, bro, let me bust some moves, and I got you," he said. "Nawl fuck that; I know you got it right now. I got shit I have to do; I need that right now, bro." I said as I pushed the money I had in my hands into my pockets. He began to go into his pocket and count out some money; he handed me $500 and said, "You crazy bro, you know I'm not going nowhere; I was gon give you your money." "Yeah, I know how you coming; I just want it once you get it not when you feel like you done taking care of all yo personal shit; then you have room left to give me mines. That's not how business works, bro," I responded. "Ok, you right bro, but fuck all that shit, you got yours, I got mines, I'm good, you good, we good," he said as he reached out to shake my hand. "Yeah, we good," I said as I shook his hand.

Once I exited the car, I saw one of the guys who also grew up around us named Rocky eating a plate full of food; bro, looking real bad out here; he used to be up getting a lot of money. All that went out the window a couple of years back when he lost his OG and his son to a fire. His OG boyfriend burned down the house one weekend on some drunk shit, trying to cook some noodles in the middle of the night. He ended up watching TV and fell asleep; sad to say, he died. But even sadder, Rocky's son begged to sleep over at his grandma's house that night. For that reason, bro been dancing with demons after that because he blames himself.

I beeped the horn to catch his attention, and he walked up to the car, "what up Kyro, you looking like real money out here," he said while smiling; his teeth were yellow and stained. "Get in, bro, hit some blocks with me," I said; he opened the door to my Jeep Wrangler. Once inside, a stench of cheap beer that most hood hypes drank hit my nose; I also noticed he had on a big, black, dirty hoodie. In my mind, you could see the dirt on his skin. I was thinking, "I know this nigga hot as hell; it's the middle of the summer"; I feel for bro, but what came out of my mouth was,

"What's to you, bro? You know I got love for you like no other; you gon always be my brother, I hope you know that. You talking about I'm looking like money, I would not for you, I remember when I first saw you getting to it, I wanted that, I wanted to get money too, you told me if this what I really wanted to do, come up with $50, and you was gon put me in tune with you big cousin and show me how to work a scale and bag up. I was like 12-year-old, bro; I remember that shit like it was yesterday; I ran home praying mama had $50 when she said she did and actually gave it to me, I shot out the house and ran back to your crib," I said as I made a right at 71st. "I know you going through it; I love you my nigga, and only want the best for you. Honestly, you played a big part in who I am today, you have to get yourself together, real shit. I'm here to support you with whatever you need. I want to see you back on top winning; this shit hurt my heart seeing you like this," I looked over, and he was sitting there with his head down; he finally responded, "It's hard, bro; I appreciate that, bro." He lifted his head and looked me into my eyes, damn it looked like he wanted to cry; I reached into my pocket and gave him $200. "I know this not much, but I love you; once you get clean, I will help you get your CDL," I told him.

My phone began to ring. It was Keazy, "This is a collect call from Kevin Watson, from Cook County Jail to accept charges press 1." "Yooo, what's good bro, what you on," Keazy said. I responded, "Shit bro thinking to myself why you have not called me in some days, but I'm out here in traffic, I'm in the car with Rocky, you on speaker too." "Yooo Rocky, what's good bro," he responded. "Shit, just trying to get through the day," Rocky replied. "Hell yeah, you know that. Hey Kyro, you hear me? We been on lockdown, the deck went up over some fuck shit, I miss yo bitch ass," he said while laughing. "I miss your ass too my nigga; what they talking about with trial," I asked. "I really don't know, you know how these people be playing crazy with a nigga, anyway good looking on the bread you laid on my OG for my lawyer," he responded. "You know it's all love bro, hold on Keazy," I said as I pulled back up on Maplewood to drop Rocky off. "Don't forget what I said, Rocky," I told him before he exited my car; even though Rocky didn't respond, his body language told me he accepted my offer. Once Rocky got out, I pulled off.

I continued speaking with Keazy, "Yooo aye bro, what you got going on with Shardo," I asked. "Man, his ass a bitch bro, the nigga told me he was gon put some bread towards my lawyer, so I had sis pull up on him, the nigga didn't even pick up, so when sis told me what he did, I called him myself, but he never answered the phone, I'm already getting lied on, I don't have time to get lied to, whole time what really pissed me off is the fact my people went out they way to pull upon him. Also, it's not that he didn't do it or couldn't do it. It's more the fact he said he was gon do it and didn't do it; the nigga gave me his word, bro, but that's the situation; why you ask me that anyway," he asked. "I was on the side of fool some hours ago; he brought you up and sooks but don't, he didn't tell me all that, he told me you asked for some bread towards your bout that shit; I made him kick out $500,

I'm gon match and send you a G, who you want me to send it to," I asked. "That's why I love you, my nigga; send it to my BM, bro," he said while laughing. "Have her send me her cash app; how much do you owe your lawyer," I asked. "I'm gon have my BM stand on top of that today, bro, and I owe my lawyer about $8,000," he responded. "Ok, you know I be busy as hell bro, but no matter what I'm doing, I'm gon pick this phone up, you know I be looking forward to your calls my nigga, I can't wait until you come home. I got some shit in the mix on some legal shit that can put you in a position to take care of you and yours; give me some days; I'm gon pull up on OG and lay $3,000 on her for the lawyer," I replied. "Good looking on that, bro; you know my OG got much love for you, bro, no lie ain't no telling where a nigga head space and the situation would be without you, bro," he responded. "You have one minute remaining," the phone operator said. "Aye, bro, we got one minute left; you heard that? I'm gon have my BM text you her cash app. Also, I'm gon put my OG on point for you, Bro; I love you, my nigga," he said. I responded, "I love you too bro, aye when you calling back?" The operator spoke, "Thank you for using G.T.L.," the phone call ended.

1:20 P.M.

I eased on the brakes as I approached a red light at the corner of Roosevelt and California. I noticed it was almost time for Tonya's lunch break. With food on my mind, I texted my wife, "I know you're hungry with your lunch break approaching; I'm already close to downtown; if so, what do you have a taste for?" Tonya worked as an insurance agent downtown for the last seven years. Tonya texted back, "Yes, I am. I have the taste for an Italian beef combination with Italian sausage on garlic bread lightly dipped with crushed hot peppers and cheese. Also, grab a Figi water. Can you go to Philly Best in Greektown?" I replied, "That sounds good, baby; I will text you when I pull up."

1:37 P.M.

While sitting inside Philly Best restaurant waiting for my order, two women sat two tables away from me. I noticed they kept looking over at me; I tried not to pay them any attention. "I like your shoes. What type of shoes are those," one of the women asked as she smiled. "These are Stefano Ricci Loafers; thank you for the compliment," I said as I smiled back. "Your teeth are so white; you must be a dentist," the other woman gestured, "I wish," I said while laughing. "Well, you are definitely well dressed," she added as she complimented me on my Tom Ford slacks and button-up dress shirt. "You must work around here at one of these hospitals," I said. "The scrubs gave us away, huh," one of the women said before laughing. "Yeah, we work at Stroger Hospital," the other said. "Well, I applaud all of your frontline services and would like to show my appreciation by paying for your meals," I said. "Well, we will happily accept our offer, thank you," both women said as I looked down at my phone; I received a text message from Keazy BM. The message read, "Hey, this Keazy wife; he told me to text you my cash app, so here it goes,

$Keazywife25." I instantly sent her $1,000.00, and she texted me right after, "he said thank you, and he loves you." I text back, "Tell bro, it's all love. Hit my line once he gets a chance." As I grabbed my order and began to head towards the door, I said to the two women, "Nice to meet you both. All enjoy your meal and the rest of your day."

2:00 P.M.

"Thank you baby," Tonya said as she unwrapped her Italian Beef and began to eat.

"You know I got to feed my baby," I said as I took a bite of my Italian beef. "I was thinking about what you said about me not having to cook tomorrow because you are taking Gabby and your mom out to breakfast. I want to go too baby," she responded. "Ok, that's not a problem; it will be great to have all my queens in one place at one time with me," I said as I noticed an all-white Volvo truck with black Limo tints pulling into the parking lot. "Aye baby, that's one of my clients; he got Life Insurance policies on his wife, kids, parents, and animals," Tonya said. "You said on his animals, what type of animals he have," I asked. She responded, "He has eight horses he breeds and races them. He has a $500K policy on each one of the horses. I responded, "Damn, you learn something new every day, I see. Awe yeah, since we are on this topic, I was also taking Gabby to pick out a car this weekend; I was thinking about getting her insurance at your office." She responded, "That's fine, but she's going to need full coverage, and she's also going to need her insurance. She's becoming a young woman and needs to start building her credit and understand the value of responsibility." I responded, "You right; I'm going to have a talk with her when I pick her up from school." "Well, my break is almost over anyway; let me get back to work," Tonya said as she kissed me before exiting the car and returning to work.

My phone rang; as I grabbed it and pressed accept, I noticed the screen read Kamie, "Yooo," I yelled into the phone. "Hey Kyro, how you coming," she asked. "I'm coming the right way, hoping to see you," I replied. "Well, I'm at home just stepping out of the shower; I'm hoping to see you as well," she answered. Kamie is a woman I met a few months back at a gas station; I later found out she owns a salon on 79th Street and doesn't stay too far from Gabby's school. We had dealings a few times; she knows of my daughter but does not know her name. She also knows I'm married but does not know where I work or live. "Give me a few minutes, and I will stop by," I told her. "How long do you think that's going to be," she asked. I responded, "Around 15 to 20 minutes." She replied, "OK. Don't keep me waiting, Kyro." I responded, "I won't." The call ended.

2:40 P.M.

I walked up the stairs to Kamie's front porch. I heard music playing as I approached her front door. She unlocked the door; when the door opened, there she stood. She's 5'6, with caramel skin, hazel eyes, and petite with blond dreads that were shoulder length. She wore a pink sports bra with the smallest skin-tight pink shorts that read Dior. They were gripping her frame in a way like no other.

"You like what you see," she asked as she turned around for me and smiled. "You know the answer to that question already," I replied as I smiled and entered her home. I told her, "Just to let you know, I can't stay long; I have to pick my daughter up from school." "That's cool, I have to go see my man at the county after 3:30, and I wanted some dick before I left. So we are on the same page," she said as she squatted down and positioned herself right in front of me as I sat in her front room on her couch.

She began to unbuckle my Tom Ford belt and unzipped my pants slowly. She eased my dick out and eased her mouth over as she stared me in my eyes and moaned. She began to speed it up, "take that shit off and bend that ass over this couch," I demanded. She did exactly what I asked of her; I forced my dick in her pussy from behind, just how I liked it. I began to pound her out as she screamed out in pleasure. Fuck, fuck, fuck, fuck, fuck!

3:29 P.M.

"How did school go for you today," I asked Gabby as soon as she put her seatbelt on. She replied, "It was good." I asked her, "Did you decide what car you want?" She answered, "Yes, I would like an Impala." I responded to her, "OK. I can do that; you know you are turning 18 real soon. So, I will tell you this: you need to start looking for work to support your situation; in the meantime, I will pay your car note and your insurance until your birthday. It's time you learn the value of responsibility. That said, you will also start paying your cell phone bill."

I turned right at the corner of 71st and Pulaski; Gabby told me, "I haven't told you yet, but I have an interview at Walmart next week. I wasn't going to tell you until I actually got the job." I responded to her, "That's great; I believe you are going to land the job. I also would like you to tap into your brain and come up with a business plan that's going to change the world." "I can't do that; how would I be able to tap into my brain," she asked. "Well, for starters, once you tell yourself you can't, then your brain will tell itself it can't, and walls begin to go up, but if you ask yourself how can I, what can I do, why can't I come up with or I need to come up with a great idea, then walls will begin to lay down and become roads like a highway route and begin to search for answers. Once you allow your brain to work for you, it is an amazing feeling to know you have unlocked the power of your brain; I will support you with whatever you come up with. You have to have your business plan written out or figured out. You should look back over your research and believe in your idea before you attempt to get others to believe. Please leave your mark on this world. I want you to create generational wealth within your bloodline. I want you to ponder this question: if you were to die today, what would people say about you tomorrow?" Telling her that made me think of my dream last night.

"I want you to know and understand at times, you are going to come across roadblocks, but you must not give up, even if you want to, because that is not an option. Always remember that the world changes, so move with the times. But stay in a space where things will always be around, such as death, property, transportation, and technology. Those are the four keys to life; I also want you to envision your end goal, meaning whatever idea you choose to move towards, be open to selling for a bigger profit, and jump-start your next business plan."

My phone began to ring as I pulled up to the light on 71st and Kedzie; I noticed it was my old man. "What's going on, Skool," I said. "I need your help moving some things over from my place to your mother's next week," he responded. "Do you mind if I ask what you are trying to move," I asked. "Let's just say you gon need one of your company trucks to get the job done," he said, laughing. "You know I can make that happen. Other than that, are you okay? Have you been taking your meds," I asked. "Everything alright, I'm stronger than an ox. I don't need them meds," he replied. "If you did not need them, the doctor would not have said you did. It would be best if you started taking your medication; I'm gon stop by tomorrow and make sure I also have to run something by you," I told him. "OK. Well, I'm gon be looking forward to it soon, son; love you," he responded. "Love you too, pops," I replied. The call ended. My father and my OG haven't been together for years. Both are remarried but are still great friends. They didn't share the details that led them to the point of no return, but honestly, we still manage to unite like a family when we are all around.

When I pulled in front of the house, my

dream flashed across my mind again. I saw my dead body on the ground; just the thought made my stomach ball up in knots. I looked at Gabby and said, "I love you so much; I want the best for you. I want you to ponder the conversation we had and tap into your power brain; as you know, I have a $500,000 life insurance policy in your name if anything ever happens to me. Most people make their biggest mistakes when it comes to money once they come across a lot of it. I would like you to learn about a CD account; it's a Certificate of Deposit. I would suggest that you put half of that policy over into a CD account to establish a foundation of security as a safety net. If your dreams do not succeed at the level you want them to, you will have another $500K to try it again or something else; all you have to do is tap into that thing between your ears called a brain, and I really believe you are going to be alright." She stopped me and said, "why you always talking about death, I don't like that, I don't know what I would do if something were to happen to you." I noticed her voice started to crack, and her eyes became watery. I saw on her face that she envisioned reality without me; I grabbed her, held her, and said, "I'm okay, baby girl, but this is life. No one lives forever; I'm not saying I'm going to die today or next month. I may be around for the next 40 or 50 years, but the reality is that tomorrow is never promised.

4:18 P.M.

Once I reassured Gabby that her nightmare would not become her reality anytime soon, I thought to myself, "Was that conversation too heavy for my baby girl."

I walked into my bedroom and closed the door behind me; I grabbed my safe from the back of my closet. I sat the safe on my bed and began to count the money I had made over the course of the day. After I got all the money separated and neatly stacked, I wrapped rubber bands around the $100 bills as well as the $50, $20, and $10 bills. Once I was done, I placed the stacks of money on top of the money already inside my safe.

I received a text that read, "WYA" from Nina. I responded, "OMW out the door." She replied, "I want to see U." Nina is a woman from my past with whom I used to be in love. I still have love for her, but it's nowhere near how I used to feel. But, like I said, I do have love for her, so I texted her back. "WYA," She replied, "at my house; when are you coming?" I answered, "Give me some time; I have some business I have to take care of, then I will be on my way."

8:25 P.M.

I find myself pulling up in front of Nina's crib and texting her, "Are you coming out, or am I coming in?" "You can come in; I'm still getting ready," she replied.

Two seconds after receiving her text, the front door swung open, and she motioned me to enter. I turned my car off and headed inside; once inside, I couldn't help but notice her phatt ass. As she walked into the bathroom, I noticed how her all-white Chanel bodysuit gripped her curves as if it was painted on her. I had only been in Nina's house five minutes before I got a text from Tonya, "Just thinking of you; I want you to know you are always on my mind and also in my heart; I love you so much, baby." I texted back, "I love you so much, words can't explain. I know I made the right choice when I gave you my name." After I sent that text, I thought to myself, "Why am I cheating on my wife? I know I have a good woman,"

When Nina stepped out of the bathroom, it threw that thought right out of my mind. "Damn, yo ass sexy as hell! I can also smell your ass from over here," I said. "You know that's nothing new, and it's called washing your ass," she replied. "Well, I know a lot of people wash their ass, and they don't smell as good as you," once I said that, she began to laugh. "You looking good; you must of just left the barber shop," Nina said as she rubbed her hands across my waves. "You know I have to keep my shit on point, but what up? What are you trying to get into tonight," I asked. "Drink a little, then feel you inside of me," she said, smiling as we walked down the stairs to the car. I can't go home smelling like pussy," as the words slipped out my mouth, her smile turned into a frown. Nina, unfortunately, has an anger issue and also suffers from bipolar disorder.

I hate when you bring that bitch up," she spat. "Here we go; I don't have time for this shit Nina, you know what I have going on, and that is my wife. She didn't do anything to you, she don't even know you. I ask you don't disrespect her again," I said in a firm tone as I looked her in her eyes. "I'm sorry, baby; you know how much you mean to me," she said while staring at me. "I would believe that if every time you get inside your feelings you didn't text me crazy shit; like, you hope I die, and you gon spit on me and all type of other shit. You really need to learn how to control your emotions because if something actually happens to me, you know you gon be the main one missing me," I said as I pulled into Kenwood liquor store parking lot on the Southwest and Pulaski across from Clowns Pizza place. "You know I don't mean shit I be saying. I just be wanting shit my way and you don't be going for all that shit, and it pisses me off baby. You know I love you and only you, right? I would paint the city red if anything was to happen to you," she said as we walked through the door of Kenwood. "It's all good, you know how we coming, but don't you want to put something in your stomach before you start drinking," I asked. "Yeah, let's stop on 95th and Kedzie to get some tacos," she said.

9:49P.M.

We were parked on a dark block full of greasy tacos and liquor running through our system. I had my dick halfway down this bitch throat. I was thinking to myself, "Damn, this bitch sucking this dick too good; it wouldn't be right if I didn't bend her ass over." I suggested, "Let's get in the back."

We both exited the car and headed towards the back; my phone kept blowing up as I slammed my dick in and out of her pussy from the back. I started to slow down on the fourth time my phone went off; Nina yelled out through her moans, "You bet not answer that fucking phone." I sped it up as I felt her reaching her peak.

It was the sixth time my phone went off and I was nowhere near finishing. I reached towards the front seat and flipped my phone over; it was Kystal calling. Kystal is my stepmom, which I don't look at her that way, but she is my old man's wife. "She never calls me this late," I thought to myself before I pressed answer. "Kyro, Kyro, where are you," she screamed in a panicked tone. "Why, what's up? What's going on," I asked as my dick started to go down. She continued, "Your father just had a stroke and fell down the stairs while he was on his way to the basement." After hearing those words, my heart jumped out of my body, and my head started to spin even more than the liquor already had it spinning. I responded, "Is he okay? I'm on my way." She replied, "I called 911; they are already here. They are putting him in the back of the ambulance and taking him to Little Company of St. Mary." "OK. I'm on my way," I said as the call ended.

I jumped back in the driver seat and slammed on the gas, "I have to drop you off; my old man is on his way to the hospital," I said. I was doing the dash above the legal speed limit back towards her house. Once I pulled up to her house, she looked back at me and said, "Please be careful before you kill yourself or somebody else." I was already back on the gas pedal before she could safely put her feet on the ground. My mind was racing, and I was racing. I grabbed my phone and called Tonya to let her know the news.

10:29 P.M.

As I cut through traffic like a bat out of hell, not caring who I cut off or cut in front of, I glanced into my review mirror. I noticed a car weaving through traffic as if it were trying to keep up or catch up to me. My first thought was, "Is this the police? Nawl, it can't be because they did not hit their lights yet." Even though my vision was a little blurry, I knew where I was headed.

I focused back on the destination at hand until I came to the red light at 79th and Western. The car I had seen pulled up on the side of me with three young niggas screaming out the window, talking a bunch of nothing. I squinted my eyes to try and get a good look at them when guns came out of the window. Shots started to ring out, and the first bullet came through my window and penetrated my jaw. I leaned over and slammed down on the gas; I felt another bullet hit my left shoulder. I drove right into the middle of the intersection with my head down. All I could hear was a big bang, and everything went dark. If I knew I was going to die today maybe I would have cried yesterday, only if I knew my tomorrow was never promised. **T.R.A.G.I.C.**

A Word from the Author

Unfortunately, we don't get to choose the trauma we experience throughout our lives. As you know, anything can happen tomorrow, but fortunately, we do hold the power to decide how we react to the trauma that may happen to stumble into our lives.

This is the third book that I have written, and within every book I have written and will write, I want you, the reader, to learn something from my stories that you can use in the real world and may pass down to the next generation. If you ever read one of my books and get to the end, when you flip that last page, before sitting the book down and walking away, and did not store a gem within your mental; I highly suggest you reread my words and understand the moral of the story as well as the message within the chapters. Thank you, and please enjoy the journey.

Other Works by the Author

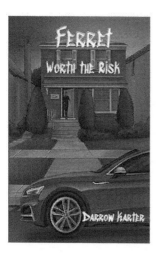

About the Book

Big C is a bonafide street dude, born and raised on the south side of Chicago. He shares twins with the love of his life, Queen. Big C invites his son to jump off the porch at a young age. Queen understood Big C was teaching his son how to protect and provide for his loved ones if he was to ever be taken out of the equation. Big C understood the power of knowledge. He instilled that into his son before he was killed. However, his son is left to use everything his father taught him growing up. Will he stay focused and keep his father's street empire an ongoing enterprise while also searching for the truth about his father's assassination?

About the Book

Kensean is a son, brother, grandson, and gang member. He grew up in a hostile environment. Their grandmother raised Kensean and his little sister Egypt after a tragic situation involving their parents. Seneca is Kensean's right-hand man; they've been around the block a few times when dealing with the streets. Growing up on the south side of Chicago, they're seeking to figure out life and everything that comes with it. Will Kensean keep his loyalty, or will he let greed steer him toward that back door?

Made in the USA
Monee, IL
07 August 2024

63430293R00028